THE golem's Latkes

ADAPTED BY

ERIC A. KIMMEL

ILLUSTRATED BY

AARON JASINSKI

marshall cavendish children

To Jacob, Emily, and Chloe
—E.A.K.

To my father. Thank you for challenging me to
draw one hundred hands when I was a kid.
—A.J.

Text copyright © 2011 by Eric A. Kimmel
Illustrations copyright © 2011 by Aaron Jasinski
All rights reserved
Marshall Cavendish Corporation, 99 White Plains Road, Tarrytown, NY 10591
www.marshallcavendish.us/kids

Library of Congress Cataloging-in-Publication Data
Kimmel, Eric A.
The Golem's latkes / by Eric A. Kimmel ; illustrated by Aaron Jasinski. —
1st ed.
p. cm.
Summary: Rabbi Judah Loew ben Bezalel visits the Emperor, leaving a new
housemaid to prepare for his Hanukkah party, but returns to find that she
has misused the clay man he created. Includes historical and cultural notes.
ISBN 978-0-7614-5904-0 (hardcover)   ISBN 978-7614-6006-0 (ebook)
[1. Golem—Fiction. 2. Judah Loew ben Bezalel, ca. 1525-1609—Fiction. 3.
Household employees—Fiction. 4. Hanukkah—Fiction. 5. Jews—Czech
Republic—Prague—Fiction. 6. Prague (Czech Republic)—Fiction. 7. Czech
Republic—Fiction.] I. Jasinski, Aaron, ill. II. Title.
PZ7.K5648Gol 2011
[E]—dc22
2010020008

The illustrations are rendered in acrylic
on wood panels.
Book design by Anahid Hamparian
Editor: Margery Cuyler
Printed in China (E)
First edition
3 5 6 4 2

mc **Marshall Cavendish** Children

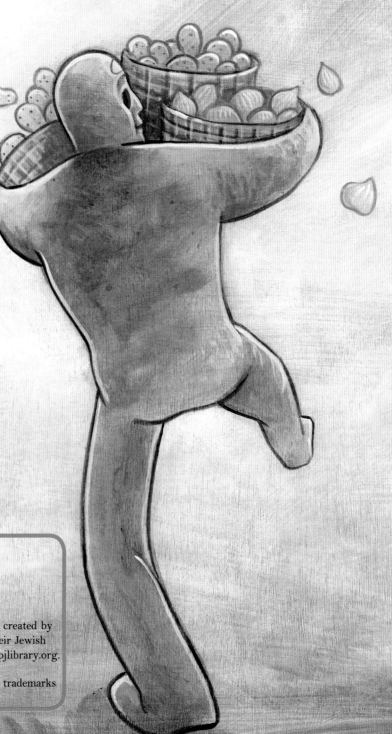

SHOFAR BOOKS

The **PJ** Library®
JEWISH BEDTIME STORIES & SONGS FOR FAMILIES

The PJ Library is an international, award-winning program created by
the Harold Grinspoon Foundation to support families on their Jewish
journeys. To learn more about The PJ Library, visit www.pjlibrary.org.

"The PJ Library" and "The PJ Library Logo" are registered trademarks
of the Harold Grinspoon Foundation. All rights reserved.

A Note from the Author

Rabbi Judah Loew ben Bezalel of Prague (1525-1609) was a prominent scholar and leader of the Jewish community. Emperor Rudolf II was the ruler of the Holy Roman Empire, which included most of Central Europe, from 1576-1612. There are many versions of the golem legend. The most famous describes how Rabbi Judah created the golem out of clay to defend the Jewish community in a time of danger. He brought the creature to life with kabbalistic rituals and incantations.

Two children's books retell the original story: **Golem** by David Wisniewski and **The Golem: A Version** by Barbara Rogasky. My story was inspired by the original legend, but also by the old tale, **The Sorcerer's Apprentice**.

Latkes are potato pancakes traditionally served during Hanukkah. **Hamantaschen** are three-cornered pastries filled with jam or poppy seeds and served during Purim, the next important Jewish holiday after Hanukkah.

The magic word on the golem's forehead is *emet*, the Hebrew word for truth (ALEF-MEM-TOF).

—E.A.K.

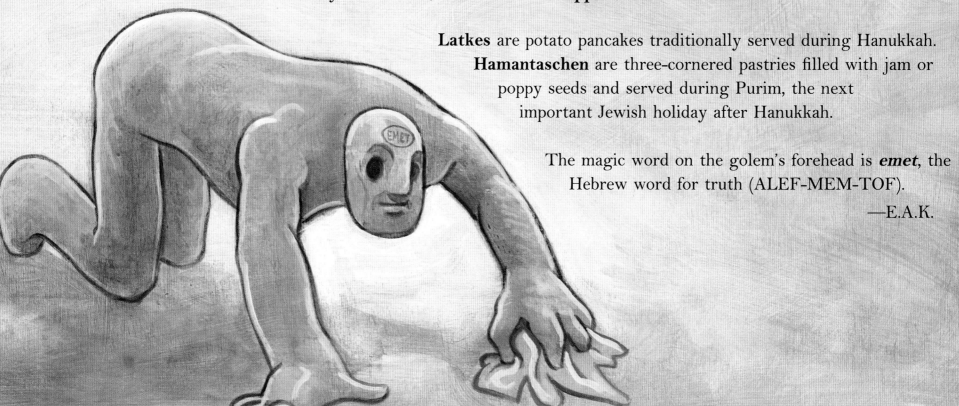

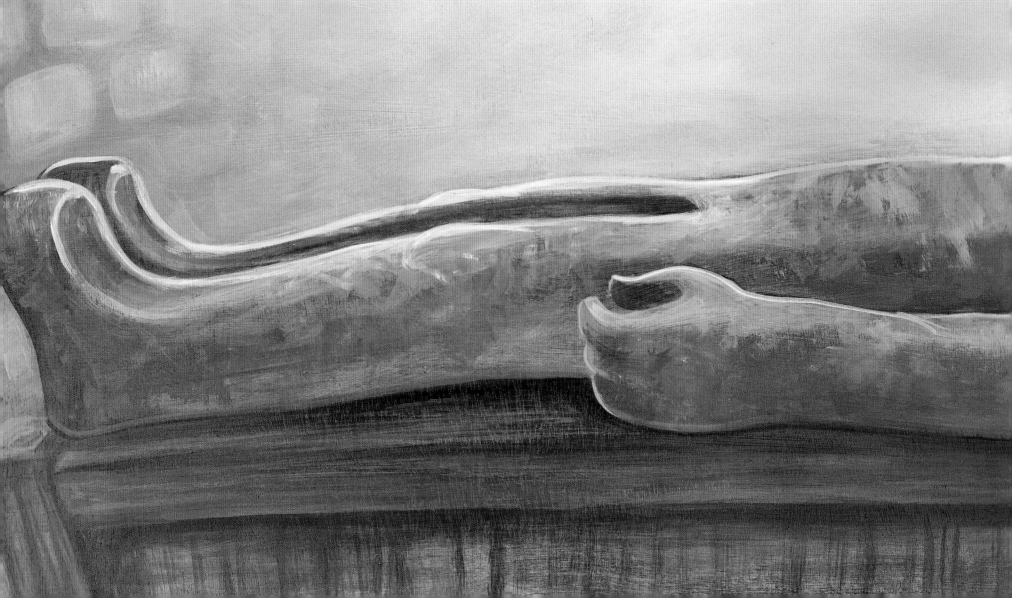

Rabbi Judah of Prague once took a great lump of clay and molded it into the shape of a giant man. He wrote a magic word on the creature's forehead. The giant came to life.

Rabbi Judah called his giant GOLEM, which means LUMP. The golem could not speak, but it could do many other things: dig, hammer, nail, paint, plaster, and cook. It could plant a garden, wash clothes, and dry and iron them. The golem could do whatever anyone asked it to do, and do it well.

There was just one problem. The golem did not know when to stop. It would keep working and working and working until someone cried, "Golem, enough!"

One winter's day Rabbi Judah found himself with much to do and little time to do it. The first night of Hanukkah would arrive that evening. He needed to show Basha, his new housemaid, how to prepare for the holiday. Then he had to leave at once to meet with Emperor Rudolf at the Royal Palace.

Rabbi Judah told Basha, "You'll sweep, dust, and mop the floor. When that's done, start making latkes. I am expecting a lot of guests tonight. We'll need plenty of latkes to feed them."

"How many should I make?" Basha asked.

"As many as you can," Rabbi Judah replied.

"What about him?" Basha pointed to the golem standing in a corner of the pantry.

Rabbi Judah hesitated. He never allowed anyone to use the golem when he wasn't present. However, Basha seemed like a levelheaded girl. She had a lot of work to do. It seemed only fair that she should have some help.

"You may use the golem," Rabbi Judah told her. "Tell him what to do and he will do it. But you must never leave the house while he is working. The golem does not know when to stop. He will keep doing whatever he is doing until someone says, 'Golem, enough!'"

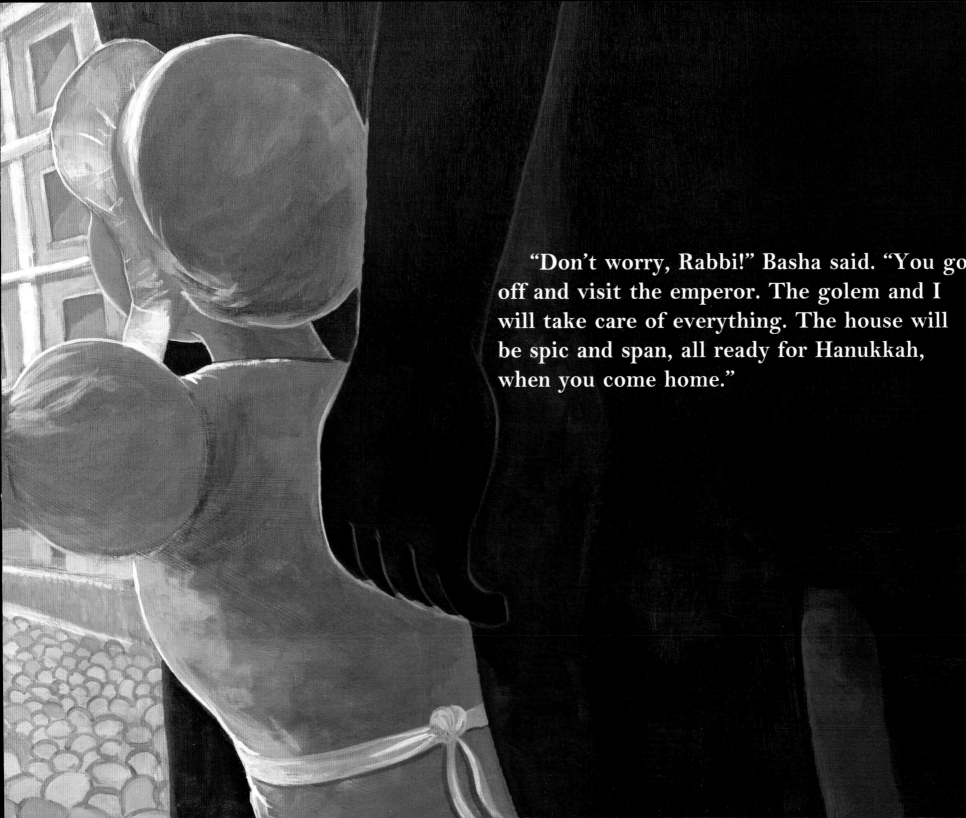

"Don't worry, Rabbi!" Basha said. "You go off and visit the emperor. The golem and I will take care of everything. The house will be spic and span, all ready for Hanukkah, when you come home."

"Well, Golem," said Basha, "let's get busy. Mop the floor."

The golem filled a bucket with hot water. He took a mop and mopped the kitchen until Basha cried, "Golem, enough!" The mop clattered to the ground. The clay giant stood still.

"I'll empty the bucket. You dust and sweep. Be careful not to break anything."

The golem began dusting and sweeping while Basha carried the bucket of dirty water outside and emptied it in the gutter. She stopped to chat with the neighbors. The golem had dusted and swept the entire house three times by the time she got back. He was getting ready to do it again when Basha cried, "Golem, enough!"

The broom clattered to the floor.
"This golem does a fine job," Basha said
to herself. "As long as he's around, I don't
have to do any work at all. Let's see if he can
make latkes."

Basha turned to the golem. "Golem, make latkes," she said.

The golem began peeling potatoes and chopping onions. He mixed them up in a great bowl with eggs, salt, pepper, and meal. He began frying latkes on the stove in a huge iron pan.

Basha tasted the first latke. "These are good!" she exclaimed. "I see you know how to make latkes, Golem. Keep working. Don't stop till I get back." She took off her apron and went to visit her friend Mary, who worked for a family living down the street.

The golem kept working. Peel. Chop. Mix. Fry. Peel. Chop. Mix. Fry. Over and over again.

Latkes filled the kitchen. Then the pantry. Then the parlor.

Peel. Chop. Mix. Fry. Peel. Chop. Mix. Fry.

Latkes pushed open the door. They tumbled into the street.

Meanwhile . . .
Rabbi Judah had a
long talk with Emperor
Rudolf.

Basha drank tea and gossiped with Mary.

The golem made latkes.
Peel. Chop. Mix. Fry. Peel. Chop. Mix. Fry.
Latkes began piling up in the streets of
Prague. They topped the city walls.
People began fleeing from the
mountain of latkes that grew higher
and higher.

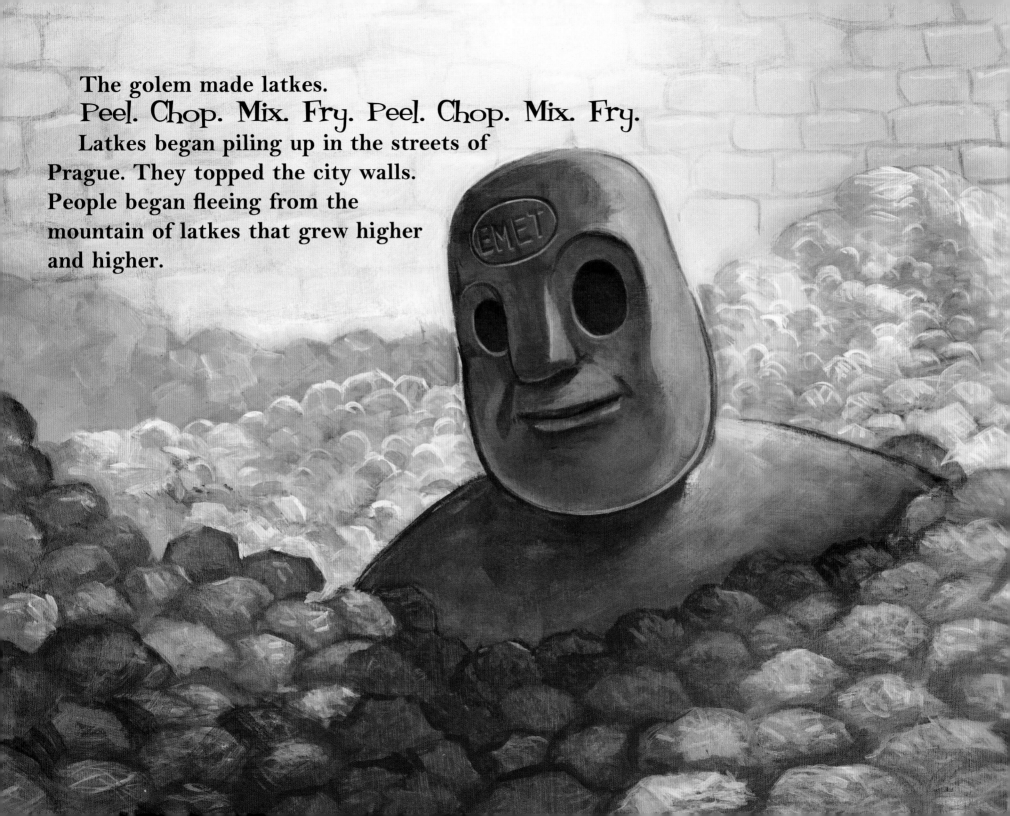

Peel. Chop. Mix. Fry. Peel. Chop. Mix. Fry.

The emperor glanced out the window.
Something on the skyline caught his eye.
 "Isn't the Church of Saint Stephen the
tallest building in Prague?"
 "It is," Rabbi Judah replied.
 "Then what's that?" Emperor Rudolf asked.

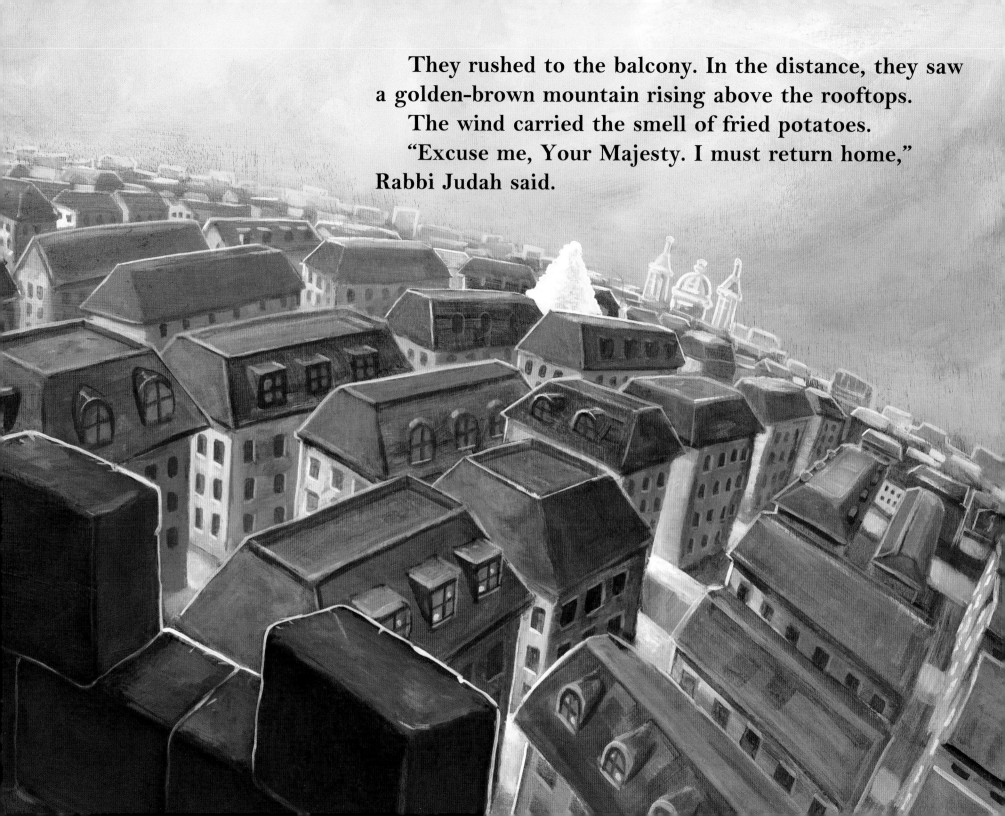

They rushed to the balcony. In the distance, they saw
a golden-brown mountain rising above the rooftops.
The wind carried the smell of fried potatoes.
"Excuse me, Your Majesty. I must return home,"
Rabbi Judah said.

Getting home wasn't easy. Latkes blocked most of the city streets.

Fleeing crowds clogged the highways.

Rabbi Judah arrived home to find latkes blocking the door to his house.

He clambered through an upstairs window. Slipping and sliding over piles of latkes, he forced his way to the kitchen. There he saw the golem standing by the stove.

Peel. Chop. Mix. Fry. Peel. Chop. Mix. Fry.

"Golem, enough!" Rabbi Judah cried.

Just then, Basha appeared.
"Where have you been?" Rabbi Judah demanded.

"Visiting my friend Mary," Basha answered. "I had such a good time, I stayed longer than I expected. Then I had to go back to borrow a ladder so I could get into the house." She looked around at the heaps of latkes. "Oh dear! What a mess! That golem must have clay for brains. He really doesn't know when to quit."

They climbed back outside. "Didn't I tell you not to leave the house while the golem was working?" Rabbi Judah said.

Basha shrugged. "I forgot. I'll do better next time."

Rabbi Judah didn't have time to scold her. "Hanukkah is almost here. Our guests will be arriving soon. What are we going to do with these latkes?"

"What else do you do with latkes?" Basha said. "Eat them!"

So they did. Rabbi Judah invited all of
Prague to his Hanukkah party. Emperor Rudolf
came with his court, bringing wagonloads of
applesauce and sour cream. People trooped
in from the countryside to join the feasting.
The party lasted eight days and nights. When
Hanukkah ended, the latkes were gone.
Every last one had been eaten.

"I don't know whether to reward you or get rid of you," Rabbi Judah told Basha after the guests left.

"Reward me," said Basha. "You're going to need me soon. Purim's coming."

"Purim!" Rabbi Judah exclaimed. "I hope you won't ask the golem to make hamantaschen!"

CAN A GOLEM MAKE HAMANTASCHEN? Basha wondered.

A faint smile crossed the golem's lips.

Hamantaschen? Why not?